A SONG OF REVERIE

Also by Suneé le Roux

The Reverie Flash Fiction Series

A Spark of Reverie
A Flight of Reverie
A Song of Reverie
A Whisper of Reverie

Standalone Short Stories

Spirit Caller

The Mythical Menagerie Series

Myth Hunter
Myth Keeper
Myth Maker
Myth Bringer

Keeper of Exotic Animals
Becoming Keeper

A Song of Reverie

A FANTASY FLASH FICTION COLLECTION

Suneé le Roux

AUTHOR'S NOTE

Every month, as a special treat for my newsletter subscribers, I use to write a little flash fiction story - something that's very short (almost always under 1000 words, and at times even less than 500 words), and something that was sparked by my love of fantasy. The magic in these stories can range from the epic sword and sorcery kind, to the often overlooked magic that can turn a mundane situation into something a little more unusual. This collection contains some of these stories. I hope you enjoy them.

If you're new to flash fiction, might I suggest you read this book slowly. It's not meant to be devoured in one sitting. Give the stories a chance to breathe - I promise you'll appreciate them more this way!

This book makes use of UK English spelling and syntax.

TABLE OF CONTENTS

THE FORBIDDEN HATCHLING

O wain wiped a trickle of sweat from his brow. Somewhere deep down below in the bowels of the fortress, some poor grunt was diligently stoking the fire that ran through the piping hidden behind thick stone walls all the way to the Hatchery, high up in a tower, where Owain now stood perspiring as he scanned this season's batch of candidate eggs.

The harvest must have been good fifty years ago, because the shelves in this wing of the Hatchery were filled to the brim with rainbow-coloured eggs the size of Owain's head, some smooth as silk, others jagged and coarse enough to grate skin off, but all glittering like forbidden treasure in the warm glow of the lamp swinging overhead. Having had the required amount of time to grow within those protective domes, the heat would now entice the little dragonets inside to finally emerge.

Owain's heart fluttered at the thought. He'd been apprenticed to the Master Hatcher for almost a year now and was yet to see a hatching. Dragons were a long-lived species and, under normal circumstances, their eggs could take as much as a century to fully develop. But ever since the legendary Grigor the Great had slain the dragon queen and subjected the beasts to slavery, fighting as war mounts in the Warlord's endless conflicts, the Hatchery had been charged with propagating dragons as fast as possible. The previous hatching had been almost two years ago. A fine batch of fighters, Master Dafydd had called them.

Movement caught Owain's eye, and he gasped as a gold-flecked emerald egg started trembling. The air crackled, as if a lightning storm were brewing.

"Master!" Owain shouted, fumbling for his leather gloves. "Come quickly!"

A loud CRACK rent the air as the egg splintered and split open. Owain's hands trembled as he carefully pried the shell's pieces apart to reveal the dragonet inside.

His breath hitched in his throat. Delicate iridescent wings unfurled as the tiny creature wobbled onto unsteady legs. Its scales were not the traditional hues of fiery red or obsidian black Owain had been taught to expect, but a luminescent silver that shimmered in the low light. The creature's eyes were large and intelligent and sparkled with an ancient wisdom.

Owain's heart swelled with a mixture of emotions – awe, wonder, and a profound sense of protectiveness. The dragonet reached out a clawed talon and gripped one of Owain's fingers in its tiny palm, and the apprentice knew immediately that an unspoken connection had formed between them, even as he heard his master's gasp behind him.

Owain turned to see Master Dafydd's face pale.

"A white hatchling!" the Master Hatcher hissed. "We must kill it now, before it's too late."

"Why?" Owain asked, alarmed. "We've waited fifty years for it to hatch!"

"And the dragons have waited centuries," Master Dafydd spat. "That, my young apprentice, is a queen, and we cannot let her live."

Ice clawed down Owain's spine. He glanced at the dragonet, who was watching them attentively, as if it understood every word they said. "It's just a baby. What harm can it do?"

"It will grow, and it will resist servitude, and it will inspire the rest of its kind to rebel against us. It must die now." Master Dafydd's hands shook as he glared at the dragonet. "Keep that thing contained. I will be right back with a dragon's bane potion."

Owain nodded, swallowing nervously. He listened until his master's stomping footsteps faded away, and then he turned back towards the dragonet. The hatchling teetered, unsteady on its feet, and Owain steadied it instinctively. He swallowed back a sob as the baby dragon nuzzled his gloved hand affectionately.

"No," Owain whispered. "This is wrong. It's just a baby."

All his life Owain had watched the dragon riders set out to war, his father at their head. He'd wanted to be one of them too, at first. But as he grew older, what had once seemed normal began to trouble Owain. He'd seen how the warriors treated their dragons – like dumb beasts, beating any signs of dissent out of them until they had reduced the magnificent creatures to nothing more than carrier mules, albeit ones that could tear a horse limb from limb. Dragons mated for life, but partners were separated and died as the Warlord saw fit, and the sole egg a female produced during her lifetime was harvested as soon as it was laid and taken to the Hatchery. Instead of becoming a warrior, Owain had apprenticed to the Master Hatcher, hoping that, somehow, he could make a difference in the dragons' lives.

And now, perhaps he could.

Owain took a deep breath. Then he scooped the dragonet into his arms and tucked it underneath his cloak, wincing as the hatchling's body heat burned against his chest. A soft vibration, almost as if the little creature were purring, thrummed against his ribcage as it snuggled in closer and a smell like burnt metal reached Owain's nose.

His heart lurched into his throat as he heard Master Dafydd stomping up the stairs again. He looked around. There was nowhere to hide, and nowhere to escape.

Except through the window.

Owain hesitated only a moment before he threw the window open. A cool breeze ruffled his hair as he leapt into the sky, the dragonet still cradled in his arms. The hatchling screeched, and an answering roar shook the night.

As they plummeted towards the ground, the sound of enormous wings flapping suddenly filled the air. Owain cried out as huge talons wrapped around his body, wrenching his fall to a stop. He looked up at the dragon who had caught him. It was his father's mount, the chain it had been bound with dangling from its neck.

An alarm rang out, but Owain's lips curled into a smile. The Hatchery dwindled below as the dragon soared higher, carrying the erstwhile apprentice and his precious cargo towards freedom and the hope of a better future.

WORTHY

"You don't have to do this."

Satya stood on the edge of the precipice, letting her eyes follow the rope tied to a stake driven into the rock, across the chasm and all the way to the stone pillar on which the Holy Temple of Ascension glowed with the rosy tint of dawn. A breeze ruffled her dark hair as the taut rope swayed slightly. "Yes, I do."

Beside her, Alani sighed. "Can't you at least wait until the wind's settled?"

Satya shook her head. "This year's crop of acolytes will be here within the hour. It's now or never." Anticipation fluttered in her chest. Soon, she'd know if she was worthy.

If not, she'd be dead.

She turned when she felt Alani's warm hand squeeze her own. Her sister's eyes were dry, but Satya felt the tremor in her grip.

"You don't have to prove anything to me."

"I know," Satya said. She pulled her hand from her sister's and took a deep breath.

Then she stepped onto the rope.

It shifted beneath her, and Satya's heart lurched into her throat. She heard Alani's stifled gasp as her gaze fell to the sheer drop far below. The chasm was so deep, the bottom was lost in darkness. For a moment, Satya imagined her body tumbling into those depths.

She clamped her jaws together and straightened her arms out, lifting her eyes back towards the temple. "Balance. Courage. Determination," she whispered the mantra through gritted teeth. The rope steadied beneath her feet.

She could do this.

"Wait!" a voice called out and Satya winced. She didn't need to look over her shoulder to know who it was. She needed the Witness to verify her crossing, but she'd hoped to be further along before he spotted her. The old man would stop her if he could.

"Wait!" he shouted again. "This attempt is not sanctioned!"

"She's already on the rope," Alani called out, her voice shrill. "Her fate is in the hands of the gods now!"

"But she's Navir!" the Witness protested.

Satya swore under her breath. She'd had enough of being judged by her clan, her fate decided by the random act of being born. Her people deserved better than that. She deserved better than that.

The rope wavered and suddenly it was all she could do not to plummet to her death. For one endless teetering moment, Satya stared into the abyss, contemplating the easy option. She could so easily be rid of it all – the shunned eye contact, the way people talked over her, the revulsion scrawled across their faces if she accidentally touched someone. As if she was no one. As if she didn't matter.

"Balance. Courage. Determination." The rope's swaying slowed, and Satya swallowed her fear down.

She lifted her eyes towards the temple. Legend said only the worthy would ascend, and every year on this day hundreds of acolytes proved themselves unworthy by falling to their deaths long before they reached the shimmering shrine. Satya didn't know what she'd find there, but it had to be better than what was here.

She could do this.

If the Witness said anything else, she didn't hear

it. She didn't hear the crowds gather to watch the Holy Ceremony of Crossing or their outraged cries. She didn't hear the acolytes howl in frustration, fearing their one chance thwarted. And she didn't hear the astonished cheering as she walked across the chasm and set foot upon the temple grounds, the first to have done so in a hundred years.

Someone was waiting there for her.

Hands trembling, Satya stumbled to her knees in front of the glowing woman, her eyes downcast.

"Rise and welcome, Sister."

Satya lifted her eyes. The woman smiled kindly and offered her hand. Uncertainly, Satya took it, and gasped as the woman pulled her to her feet and wrapped her in an embrace. A tear leaked down Satya's cheek as a warmth she had never felt before enveloped her.

"Balance. Courage. Determination," the woman whispered. "You are worthy."

When the woman pulled away, Satya felt different. She stood straighter. Her doubts were gone. And her skin glowed.

Astonished, she gaped at the woman.

"Yes," her Sister said. "You are one of Us now." She squeezed Satya's hand in encouragement, her gaze straying towards the promontory and the throngs in the distance. "Go. Show them who you are."

Satya's lips quirked into a smile. And then she shot into the sky, arched effortlessly across the ravine, and landed in the midst of the crowd. Onlookers screamed, acolytes fell to their knees, a few people turned and ran down the hill; all overwhelmed by the sudden presence of a goddess in their midst. All but one.

Alani stood at the edge of the cliff, her face painted with rapt awe. Then she smiled, and her lips formed the words: "I knew it."

Satya turned to the surrounding people.

"I am Satya of the Navir," she said, for the first time not ashamed or afraid. For once, everyone's attention was on her. She looked every one of them in the eyes, before she wrapped her presence around them in a comforting embrace, feeling their fear abate as they reached for her touch.

"And I am here to bring Balance."

THE GHOST OF FROSTFELL FUTURE

Elemetheus awoke from his long sleep, and sighed. Another Frostfell, another ungrateful soul to prod towards repentance.

It was the same thing every year. Some unlucky sod was heading towards an unhappy ending, and it was Elemetheus' responsibility to show them the error of their ways. Inevitably, the penitent was contrite for a day or two, perhaps even until the first moonrise of the new year, but then they predictably returned to their former ways.

It was a waste of Elemetheus' afterlife.

But, unless he wanted to fade into obscurity – and a shudder ran through Elemetheus' incorporeal body at the thought – he had to stick to the terms of his contract. He sighed again. Better crack on with it.

Something felt different this time, though. Normally, he would awake from his slumber beside the rapscallion, but this time there was only him. He glanced around and frowned as he recognised his marbled surroundings. Was this his mausoleum? Indeed, there on a dusty shelf sat the alabaster urn that contained his mortal remains.

Behind him, someone cleared his throat. Elemetheus spun around, startled.

"George!" he exclaimed. "You nearly sent me to the Beyond again!"

His colleague's wispy face twisted into a grimace. "Sorry, old boy," George said. "You know how it is."

Elemetheus frowned. "How what is?"

George shrugged. "This. The gig." He gave an exasperated huff at Elemetheus' uncomprehending stare. Then he cleared his throat again, lifted his hands and wiggled his fingers and, in a voice much deeper and more majestic than usual, he pronounced: "Behold thy past and repent!"

A gust of wind nearly knocked Elemetheus over. His ethereal limbs froze into place as visions of days gone by flashed before his eyes. He saw himself, newly raised as Ghost, his eyes glimmering with anticipation. He felt anew the rush of victory as his first sinner promised to atone for his wrongdoings. Past Elemetheus' joy shone on his face with every vision he delivered, every person whose path he altered, and Elemetheus felt a keen sense of loss as the vision faded and he found himself alone in the mausoleum again.

"I was naïve then," he said aloud, his voice echoing in the oppressive space. "I thought I could make a difference."

"And you did." Elemetheus' gaze snapped towards the tall spirit floating next to his urn. Solaria's face was pinched with disapproval. "At first."

"Please don't tell me you're here to show me the error of my ways," Elemetheus groaned. "I did what I could, but nothing ever changed. They saw their futures, and they continued as before."

"Not all of them," Solaria said.

"Most of them," Elemetheus snapped. "And they deserved what they got, if you ask me."

His colleague pulled herself to her full, impressive height, her bold brows drawn into a fierce scowl. She lifted an imperious finger.

Elemetheus rolled his eyes. "Here we go again," he sighed.

"Behold thy present and repent!" Solaria intoned, and Elemetheus braced himself as a vision assailed him, slamming his body up against the cold marble wall.

He saw himself, and gasped at how bent his shoulders were, how many creases marred his forehead, how hard his agate eyes seemed. Elemetheus winced as Present Elemetheus sneered 'And they deserved what they got, if you ask me'. Shame flushed through his body as the vision faded and he stood once again alone in his deserted mausoleum.

He sagged up against the wall. How could he have let it come to this? How could he have given up hope so easily? What would happen to him if he continued in this way?

There was only one way to find out.

He braced himself, and then whispered: "Behold thy future and repent."

The vision folded across him like a veil. He shivered as an icy wind wafted through the cemetery. The rubble of his torn down mausoleum lay littered around his feet. A young man stumbled past – his gaunt features unable to hide the familial resemblance – and fell into an open grave. Elemetheus shuddered. Of Future Elemetheus, there was no sign.

The vision released him, and Elemetheus dropped to the cold floor, sobs wracking his body. He had always feared oblivion, and now it seemed his callousness would bring about not only his own end, but the downfall of his line as well.

Unless…

Elemetheus glided to his feet. His hands balled into fists. He could make a change. He could stop that future from ever coming to pass. And he knew just what to do.

There was a young man bearing a striking resemblance to the Ghost of Frostfell Future who merited a visit…

THE SIREN'S CALL

K apheira watched her prey toss the little sailboat's anchor into the choppy waters above the migratory sea lane favoured by whales heading towards the dying seas. The man scurried around, his mop of curly hair tangling with the wind. She dipped below the waves again and swam closer, careful not to let the sun catch on her pearlescent scales. Better that he didn't know she was there until it was too late.

She was just about to breach the sea when the familiar thrum of Vetra's sonar pulsed against her scales. Kapheira twisted sideways just in time to see a flash of green and silver surge past her. She thrashed backwards, and lifted her head out of the water, gasping as Vetra's song hit her ears.

Blood boiled in Kapheira's veins as she glared at the harlot. Vetra had already lured five men to her cave this season and had spawned enough fry to keep the colony growing for years to come. She was influential enough that she didn't need another catch. Her intrusion could be based on nothing but spite.

Kapheira bared her teeth as she remembered what Vetra had called her, loud enough for all to hear: tone-deaf. Her hands shook at the memory of the whispers following in her wake: a siren who repelled instead of enamoured.

That was why she was here today, stalking this man in his little boat. To show Vetra, to show all of them, that she could catch someone too.

And now Vetra was singing.

Enmity bitter in her mouth, Kapheira turned her attention back to the boat. Her eyes widened. The man was not hanging over the railing, staring smitten into the siren's alluring eyes. He was not even paying her any attention. He sat in the bow, a thin stick in his one hand, dragging it across something white on his lap that flapped in the breeze. Every now and again, he stood up and dipped a transparent container in the blue water, before sitting back down again, all the while heedless of Vetra's song.

Kapheira glanced at her rival. Vetra's elegant brows were furled downwards in a glare that resembled the fury of a cyclone. Her cheeks were blotched and red, her notes beginning to waver. Then her song stopped, the sudden silence deafening. Vetra screeched in fury, a sound more seagull than siren, and dived into the deep. Only a trail of bubbles marked her passing.

Incredulous, Kapheira looked at the man again. He was still engrossed in whatever he was doing, oblivious of how close to death he'd come.

She watched him until he pulled the anchor up and sailed off, and she watched him every day after when he returned to the same spot, always in the bow with his little stick and his containers. She saw how the skin on his face and arms bronzed in the sun, and how excited he was when the whales came. She studied how the wind played with his hair, how it caressed his face, and she envied its brazen touch when all she could do was watch.

And then, one day, the sailboat didn't come.

Kapheira bobbed between the waves until the sun painted the ocean as red as her longing.

When she knew for sure that he would not return, Kapheira followed the trail his boat had left for so many days, dodging shark nets and fisheries, until she found the sailboat moored beside a beach tucked between two clifftops. Gentle waves lapped against a little whitewashed house, and there, with his feet in the sand, stood the man, looking out across the ocean.

Not long ago, Kapheira would have lifted her voice in a song to lure him to her. She would have thought only of the moment's pleasure, the children it would bring to secure her status in the colony, and the white of his eyes as she drowned him afterwards.

But now... Now Kapheira swallowed the pain away as her tail cleaved in two and the salty ocean scoured the scales from her newly formed legs. She filled her lungs with fresh air, and for the first time in her long life, set foot on land.

She studied the man closely, and her heart leaped into her throat the moment he noticed her walking towards him, warm water dripping from her cascading hair. In his eyes she saw recognition, as if he had been watching her too all this time, and no trace of fear. His gaze never left hers, and Kapheira finally understood how easily men could walk to their doom.

When only the width of a whisper separated them, Kapheira stopped, suddenly self-conscious. Would he run from her voice? Would he chase her away, like the last man she had tried to ensnare? She was sure her heart would burst if he did.

She opened her mouth to speak, but the man placed a finger on her lips. He smiled and shook his head, placing his hands across his ears, then shrugged and shook his head again.

And at last, Kapheira realised why no siren's song could lure this man.

He gently reached for her hand, and she let him pull her from the beach. Together they walked towards his little house as the sunset faded across the ocean behind them, silence wrapped comfortably around them.

GUARDIAN OF THE FOREST

The hunter shifted his weight, slowly peering out from behind the trunk of a tall fir tree. Dappled light filtered through the dense canopy from above, illuminating a large brown bear standing next to a stream beside a small fall filling the glade with the sound of rushing water.

A salmon leaped into the air, straining against the current. With lightning-fast reflexes, the bear caught the fish in its maw. With its catch still in its mouth, the bear waded back to the shore. The man grunted as the animal tossed the fish into a woven basket at the water's edge.

Slowly, the hunter hefted his spear. The bear's head lifted, its gaze flicking towards the man's hiding place as it sniffed the air. With power born from a fervent hatred, the hunter hurled the weapon at his target.

The bear lunged to the side, narrowly missing the spear. The hunter charged out from behind the tree, darting towards the weapon now embedded into the mossy riverbank. He needed to end this! His fingers narrowly missed closing around the spear's shaft as he felt the animal's arms wrap around his torso. The man yelled as he was lifted into the air and tossed across the stream, landing hard on the bank on the far side. Surging to his feet, he turned towards his prey again.

A woman stood on the other side of the stream, her arms folded across her chest, her thick brown hair cascading down her back. "Why are you trying to kill me, wolf?" she asked, eyes blazing.

"I'm no wolf," the hunter spat, his hands clenching into fists.

"Funny. You smell like one."

The man suppressed a growl. "Shifting is an abomination. No man should wear the skin of a dumb brute!" The woman's face softened into a look of pity, and his vision clouded with anger. Snarling in fury, the hunter stormed across the river.

The woman's shape blurred and the man ducked as the enormous brown bear swiped at him. Pain exploded against his shoulder as he was battered towards the ground. Twisting, he fell onto his back and grunted as the bear held him down with one massive paw. Fear iced down his spine as the animal opened its maw, revealing razor-sharp canines, and roared, the stench of fish warming the hunter's face.

His body reacted instinctively, surrendering to primal forces embedded within his very being. An animal howl escaped his lips as his muscles rippled, adapting to elongating bones rearranging themselves, and thick fur sprouted across his skin. His lips parted in a snarl as the bear retreated, and the great grey wolf bounded to its feet.

A spear was pointed at its heart. The wolf tensed.

"Breathe," the woman said, once again in her human form. "Just breathe."

The wolf took a startled step backwards as the world around it expanded. The earthy fragrance of moss and damp soil scented the air, along with the crisp aroma of the living trees towering above, and the salty scent of the river rushing past. Its ears caught the rustle of small creatures scurrying through the underbrush and of wings flapping unseen above. It blinked as colours more vivid than the man could ever have imagined refined every shape of the surrounding woods.

The wolf's mind reeled as it realised it was

connected to the pulsing heart of the forest, and every living being within it.

"Now do you understand?"

The wolf sat back on its haunches, overwhelmed.

The woman lowered the spear and tossed it to one side. She bent down until her eyes were level with the wolf's. "Come back to your human self. Remember who you were."

The man groaned as his body shifted back into its familiar shape. "I don't want to remember," he admitted. The loss of his newfound senses was like the absence of a severed limb.

The woman placed a hand on the man's shoulder. Her touch was warm and gentle. "We are the link between man and nature," she said. "It's up to us to protect the balance. Will you join us?"

The erstwhile hunter hesitated, caught between the ingrained beliefs of his past and the undeniable truth before him. After a prolonged pause, he nodded.

"Come on, then," the woman said, helping him to his feet. A smile lit her face. "You have much to learn."

Her shape shimmered, as did his, and then the bear and the wolf loped deeper into the forest, together.

THE POTION'S PRICE

A bell tinkles as I open the door. The small apothecary smells of sage and cinnamon and the dark wood-panelled walls are lined with shelves filled with jars containing all sorts of powders and potions. I hesitate in the doorway.

The woman behind the counter looks up, her green-eyed gaze assessing. "What's her name?" she asks, wiping her hands on her apron.

"How did you...?" I stammer.

"Close the door behind you," she says, and I pull it shut. A bead of sweat runs down the back of my neck. Is it warm in here? "You have that look about you," the woman continues, her long black hair reflecting the soft glow of the candle she lights. It casts eery shadows across the walls and I wonder again if I should have come.

She beckons me closer.

Hesitantly, I walk up to the counter. "Isabella," I say. Her name lodges in my throat, a sob I try to swallow down as I remember her smile, the warmth of her hand in mine, the endless summer days together. I bite the inside of my cheek, tasting the bitterness of blood. My name was no longer on Isabella's lips, but hers would always be on mine.

The woman nods. She pulls a granite mortar and pestle closer. "It will cost you."

"Anything," I breathe, sliding my credit card across the counter.

The woman nods again, her eyes holding mine for a few moments. Then she swipes the card and hands it back to me. I don't look at the amount as I accept the transaction.

She turns and pulls various jars off the shelf behind her, placing them all on the counter before me. I don't know what half of them are. A pinch of something brown goes into the mortar, followed by two rose petals and a dash of glittering crystalline dust. She chops up the roots of a weed and presses two drops of its oil into the mortar. My nose wrinkles at the stench.

"Can you hand me that?" she asks, pointing at the wall next to me.

I reach for a vial of clear liquid and hear her say: "And the one next to it." I place the flask of green liquid beside the vial on the counter.

The woman carefully measures four drops of the green and adds it to the mixture. "Tears of a weeping willow," she explains as I look curiously on. Then three of the white. "Morning dew collected at dawn's first light, to symbolise new beginnings."

For the first time in months, I let myself hope.

"I'll need a lock of your hair," she adds, pulling a small knife from a drawer. I lean towards her. A faint earthy smell hovers around the woman, like wet grass and fresh mud. She snips a piece of my hair off and puts it in the mortar. Then she grinds it up and mixes it all together.

Finally, she takes a copper spoon from the drawer, gathers the concoction on it, and holds it out to me. My eyes water as a pungent smell assails my nostrils.

I take the spoon from her. I hadn't believed the rumours at first, stories whispered in bars late at night after all but the most hopeless souls had left, of a dark-haired woman with knowing eyes who could brew happiness and hope and sell it to you in a bottle. They'd said she could craft revenge too, inflict curses and nightmares upon your enemies, or distil luck so potent your own mother would have trouble believing your good fortune.

But I was here only for love.

Isabella doesn't want me anymore, and no amount of pleading has won her back. I would give anything to hold her in my arms again, to mend this broken heart. I've tried everything in my power to regain her affection, but all I received in return was disdain. Now it was time to try something else.

I put the spoon in my mouth. Swallow its bitter contents. It leaves an acrid aftertaste and a tingling sensation on my tongue. I wipe my lips with the back of my hand.

At first, nothing happens. Then my eyes start watering and I feel tears running freely down my cheeks. I drop the spoon as a sharp pain shoots through my chest, as if my heart is being ripped in two. I stagger backwards, casting an angry glance at the woman. The witch! Has she poisoned me?

She watches calmly from behind the counter, her arms folded across her chest and her eyes as enigmatic as ever.

Slowly, the pain recedes, and a warm sensation envelops me. A smile flutters across my lips. It feels as if a weight has been lifted.

I look around the room. It seems to be an apothecary's shop. Why am I here again?

The woman behind the counter blows the burning candle out and starts cleaning up. She'd made quite a mess with her mortar and pestle. She glances at me. "I'll send your regards to Isabella."

I frown. "Who?" I asked, confused.

The woman's smile is as cryptic as her next words. "The price has been paid in full. Close the door behind you when you leave."

I exit the apothecary with the sensation of having lost something, but, as a fresh breeze tangles in my hair, I saunter away with a lightness in my step. It feels like a new beginning.

ONCE UPON A TIME

Once upon a time, in a faraway land, a princess lay asleep in a castle overgrown with thorny brambles. For a hundred years – or so the storytellers say – she dreamed of the prince who would break the curse and release her from the spell with true love's single kiss.

And for one hundred years, Mildred – the stories never mention her, by the way – watched over the sleeping girl. She bathed the princess' comatose body, spooned a sloppy yet nourishing porridge into her slack mouth every morning and every evening, and washed the soiled bedclothes when nature ran its course. Mildred swept the room and kept any over-enthusiastic creepers away and, from time to time, removed the corpses of the hopeful suitors ensnared within the castle's spiky barrier.

All this Mildred did with patience and fortitude because, you see, it was she who had doomed the poor girl to this unfortunate fate. Yes, yes, there was the matter of the thirteenth witch who had wanted the princess dead for the slight of not being invited to her naming feast, but really, if Mildred had been any better under pressure, she would never have deflected the curse with such an arduously long sentence. As things stood, the girl would wake up with her family long dead and her castle deserted. The least Mildred could do was keep her enchanted body clothed and fed so that, when the time came, the right young man could be persuaded to kiss the poor sun-deprived thing.

Mildred was watching just such a young man right then, marching up towards the castle gates. From her vantage point at the window of the princess' tower, she saw him flourish his gleaming sword – nearly slicing his own ear off in the process – and hack at the brambles as if mere force could win the day. She rolled her eyes. She'd wanted someone better for her princess – was it too much to ask for a prince whose wit outstripped his brawn? – but to be honest, time was up, and she could do with a change of scenery.

With a flick of her wrist, the thorns shrunk under the ardent young man's blows and – almost as if destined by fate – the castle gates swung open before his self-assured stride.

Mildred's pulse quickened as she cast a glance across the room. There lay the princess under her canopied bed, her blonde curls gleaming and her cheeks as rosy as a quick pinch could make them. In the corner stood the spindle that had failed to kill her – perhaps Mildred should have removed it, and she'd tried once or twice, but had been prevented by a certain sense of sentimentality. After all, if not for the girl's foolish curiosity, Mildred would never have known if her counter spell had been effective, so many years ago.

Footsteps pounded on the spiral staircase and Mildred had just enough time to cast a glamour upon herself before the prince stormed into the room. His gaze swept unseeing over Mildred and fell upon the sleeping princess, snoring ever so sweetly – thankfully, eleven others had blessed her with such grace and charm and beauty that no amount of respiratory congestion could dampen the young man's ardour. With reverent footsteps, he closed the space between them, leant down and – as butterflies pirouetted in Mildred's chest – kissed the sleeping princess' lips.

The girl's eyelids fluttered as she woke, then her

29

lovely blue eyes widened in terror and she shrieked, pushing the prince away from her. She scrambled to her feet, her face contorted in rage.

"How dare you?" she spluttered, her pallor suddenly an attractive shade of violet.

The prince's jaw fell open. "I thought... I mean..." He raked a hand through his dark locks. "You were asleep!"

"You had no right!" the girl fumed. "How dare you!"

Mildred felt it was time to intervene. The two young people gasped as she stepped out of the shadows. The prince's hand reached for his sword, but the girl gasped in recognition.

"Dear one," Mildred smiled kindly at the princess. "He is your true love."

The girl's mouth flattened into a thin, bloodless line. She shook her fist at Mildred. "You! You had no right either!" Frantically, she looked around the room, as if searching for an escape. Her gaze landed on the spindle in the corner, and a look of fierce triumph filled her eyes.

Before Mildred could so much as utter a word of magic, the princess leapt towards the spindle and – quite deliberately – pricked her thumb on its sharp point. She turned towards Mildred, strikingly beautiful in her elation, and tumbled to the cold stone floor where she lay, unmoving.

The prince peered at her. "Is she...?"

"Quite dead," Mildred said, annoyed. After all these years – after *all* she had done – this was how she was repaid? Ungrateful child!

Mildred ushered the prince out of the room. "Well, thank you for coming. Best of luck finding your next bride." She slammed the door in his baffled face and turned back towards the dead girl, tutting irritably. Huffing, she dragged the princess' body back towards the bed and heaved it up underneath the canopy. Quickly, she arranged the body so that the hair was just so, the hands rested on her heart, the dress folded flatteringly.

Mildred took a step back. There. Perfect.

For a moment, Mildred was at a loss. Now what?

Then she remembered the request she had seen in the local newspaper earlier that week. Apparently, there was a wooden puppet who wanted someone to help him become a real boy. That sounded like a challenge she could undertake.

But this time, she wouldn't do it all by herself – no! He'd have to *work* for his happily ever after.

Without glancing back at the body on the bed, Mildred turned her back on the room she had spent a century in and eagerly set out on her next adventure.

THE FERRYMAN'S FEE

From his vantage point behind an olive tree, Alkaios watched the widow seal the dead man's mouth with an *obol* that glinted promisingly in the fading light. Tears streamed down the woman's face as she placed a funerary wreath upon her late husband's head, before stepping away from the grave and letting the men from the village lower the body into the freshly dug pit. As the woman's wails filled the air, Alkaios turned his back on the proceedings and walked away, rubbing his hands in anticipation.

Later that night, with a full moon lighting his way, Alkaios returned to the grave, shovel in hand. The muscles in his arms bulged as he worked at unearthing the body. He'd long since overcome any feelings of guilt graverobbing might have evoked, but he looked up quickly when the leaves of the olive tree rustled. He peered into the dark. Only fools believed in ghosts. After a few minutes, he shrugged and continued digging. Must have been an errant breeze.

When his shovel hit something soft, Alkaios bent down and scrubbed the dirt away until he'd uncovered the pallid face of the deceased. He thrust his hand into the dead man's mouth, his fingers grasping for the token that would ensure the ferryman's goodwill.

Alkaios gasped as he pulled the coin out, the moon glinting on gold. It wasn't often that villagers sent their loved ones to the Underworld with such a costly token. The widow must have loved her husband dearly.

Alkaios pocketed the gold, whistling a jaunty tune as he filled the grave up again. He wouldn't want the widow to know her husband had been deprived of his passage to a happy afterlife. Alkaios might prey on the superstitious, but he wasn't a monster.

He fingered the gold coin in his pocket all the way home, where he rested his dirty shovel next to the door before strutting over to the loose floorboard in his kitchen. He uncovered the hiding hole and tossed the widow's coin onto the pile of others he had liberated from the village graveyard over the years. Alkaios allowed himself a moment of satisfaction. Dead people didn't need the money, and he needed to eat. It worked out pretty well, as far as he was concerned.

"You bastard!"

Alkaios spun just in time to see the widow's enraged face before the shovel hit him and everything turned black.

⊰◆⊱

His eyelids fluttered open as a pounding headache tried to split his skull in two. The first thing he noticed was the stalagmites hanging from his kitchen rafters. The second was the dog licking his face. No, make that *three* dogs.

"I'm telling you, my wife loved me! She would never have sent me here without a coin!"

Alkaios wiped the dog slobber from his face and pushed himself to his feet. He rubbed his stubbled chin as he surveyed his surroundings. He was not in his kitchen anymore, but in an immense cave with a black river running through it. A group of people were clustered on the river's banks, clamouring around a man that looked suspiciously like the one

33

Alkaios had reburied not too long ago. They were shouting at a man guarding a boat.

The dogs barked next to him and Alkaios turned to aim a kick at one of them, when his jaw dropped open. Not dogs. Dog. With three heads.

Dazed, Alkaios returned his attention to the crowd. He staggered closer, his gaze swooping past the people and across the river to the other bank. He gasped. In all the tales he had been told, the Underworld was a dismal place where shades of the deceased languished in perpetual gloom. But what he saw on the other side… A valley lush with fruit trees, shimmering with rainbows cast by the spray of countless waterfalls, basking in the golden glow of an eternal spring day. It was… Paradise.

Alkaios gulped. And if that was so, then the three-headed dog still licking his hand must be Cerberus, and the black river must be the Acheron, and the boatman must be Charon. It must all be true.

And here he was, without a coin for the ferryman.

"None of you can pay the fee, so none of you will be crossing," Charon rasped in a voice coarse as a sharpening stone running across a bronze sword. "And you have him to thank for that."

Alkaios swallowed as the crowd turned towards him. There was the widow's husband, and old Democles the baker who had passed a few months ago, and Elpis the village whore, and even little Petros, his brother who had drowned as a child nearly three decades ago and who had been the recipient of the first coin Alkaios had ever stolen, and countless others whose obols all lay hidden beneath his kitchen floor.

"Wait!" he shouted as hands grabbed him and dragged him towards the river. "I didn't know it was true! I thought it was all a lie!"

"Throw him in the water," the widow's husband

ordered. "He can spend eternity in –" The man coughed and gagged and spluttered and when he took his hand away from his mouth, he held a gold coin between his fingers.

His eyes widened. The widow's husband turned and offered the coin to Charon, who accepted it with a smile and ushered the man onto his boat.

Suddenly, everyone around Alkaios was hacking and spitting. Alkaios fell onto the cold stone floor as the hands that had held him reached for coins inside their owners' mouths. The widow must have ransacked his hoard and returned the coins to their final resting places.

The ferryman welcomed everyone aboard as Alkaios rose to his feet and dusted himself off.

He tried to join the others on the boat, but Charon whistled once and Cerberus barred his way, growling ominously. "No coin, no passage," the ferryman said as he pushed the boat away from the shore. A cheer rose as it slowly sailed towards Paradise.

Seething, Alkaios glared after the ferryman. There was no one to leave an obol in his mouth, no one to mourn his death. He was doomed to spend eternity in the Underworld, within sight of Paradise, forever out of his reach.

Alkaios slumped to the ground. He would have lived his life differently. If only he had known...

I FOUND HER

I'm about to call it a day when something glinting in the dirt catches my eye. I swap my little trowel for a brush to sweep away the loose sand, feeling my pulse quicken as a golden medallion emerges from the dust, its green and black surface mottled with age. My breath catches at the embossed design – sinuous snakes encircling the head of a roaring lion. This must have belonged to someone important.

"Over here!" The excitement makes my voice shrill.

Carefully, I keep clearing earth away. My breath hitches in my throat as my brush reveals a yellowish fragment of old bone.

The smell of cognac and greased leather assails my nose. "What do we have here?" Dr Smith leans in for a closer look. He gasps, his fingers stroking reverently across the medallion. "Do you know what this means?" I shake my head, even though he doesn't look at me. "The snakes and the lion are symbols of Ishtar, goddess of love and war. This pendant would have belonged to one of her high priestesses."

A shiver of exhilaration runs down my spine. In the three months we've been encamped here, somewhere along the Euphrates between Babylon and Uruk in what was once ancient Mesopotamia, but is now Iraq, we've uncovered nothing more sensational than pottery shards. A high priestess of Ishtar, however… That was the kind of discovery that could elevate careers.

And I was the one who found her.

Dr Smith beckons some of the other archaeology students closer and they crowd around me with their own brushes and shovels, shooting envious glances my way as they work. The sun begins to set as we carefully uncover more of the remains. The bones are brittle, but we manage to excavate most of the body. She had been tall, for a woman – over six feet, and gold threaded the scraps of cloth still clinging to her frame.

I notice something clasped within her hand. Carefully, I pry it loose. The clay tablet is the size of my palm and covered in cuneiform script – the subject of the doctoral dissertation I'm working on. I immediately recognise some of the words. My finger traces the grooves as I try to decipher the text. It looks like a poem, or perhaps a spell…

The words are harsh on my tongue, a language not meant to be spoken anymore. From the corner of my vision, I see Dr Smith's eyes widen. Strangely, he looks more alarmed than impressed.

As the last syllable fades in the sudden silence, I look up from the tablet to see a golden light blooming from inside the dead priestess' chest. I stagger backwards, hardly noticing the other students' screams as they flee, my eyes rivetted on the bones lifting from the ground, the flesh taking shape around them, the threadbare rags swirling into lustrous silk spun with gold.

And then she stands before me, flesh and blood, but more than that, more than a mere mortal. Her presence is like a storm raging against the borders of my mind. Her eyes burn into mine with the power of a thousand suns. Visions of death flash before my mind's eye: cities burning, battlefields littered with countless bodies, crows feasting, the fertile earth satiated by unending rivers of blood. And behind it all, the alluring face of the woman gazing down upon me now, smiling.

This was no priestess. This was the goddess herself.

Beside me, Dr Smith puffs out his chest. "Beautiful Ishtar," he leers, lasciviousness dripping like oil from his tongue. "Let me be the first to welcome you back."

The goddess deigns to look at him, and I tremble as her gaze releases me.

Shuddering, I pull my mind back from the brink of insanity. I remember a dusty book in a neglected part of the university library. Between its fragile pages, I had read about Inanna, an older manifestation of Ishtar; a goddess of lions and serpents.

"What did you call me?"

A goddess who had loved nothing more than bloodshed, who had revelled in the atrocities of war, and to whom the cries of the dying were like a heavenly choir.

Dr Smith falters. "Beautiful –" His voice cuts off as his eyes bulge out of their sockets. His body wracks spasmodically as he gasps for air. I gag as the smell of burning flesh reaches my nostrils. His skin charcoals, and I turn my head and empty my stomach on the dust. When I wipe my mouth, the charred remains of my mentor lie smouldering at my feet.

I feel the weight of her eyes on me again. She lifts an eyebrow.

"Inanna," I whisper.

Her mouth curls into a smile. "Let the world burn," she says. She turns on her heel and stalks off towards the setting sun, a trail of molten sand seared black behind her.

How does one stop a goddess? The world *would* burn.

And I was the one who found her.

PORTAL TO AVALON

The hiker shook her head. "Wow, it's windy up there," she said as she strode past Morgan down the hill. "Good luck if you're heading up."

Morgan's gaze swept towards the tower at the top of the steep Tor, a stark slash of brown stone against the cloudy sky. As if in warning, a gust of wind whipped her raven hair around her face, carrying the saccharine scent of Glastonbury with it. She'd consulted with many diviners, palmists, and spiritualists during her three months in town; she'd walked the ley lines and bathed in the sacred springs.

It was time.

Morgan took a deep breath and started climbing the steps leading up the hill.

That wasn't her real name, of course. Disappointingly, her parents had been deeply unoriginal when she was born, and still lacked any spark of creativity that would have made the obligatory Sunday afternoon family lunches somewhat bearable. She'd always known she was different. That she didn't belong. She'd sought her solace in books and the esoteric truths of the old myths and legends, and when a fortune teller at a medieval festival had gazed into a crystal ball and breathlessly illuminated Morgan's ancient past, she'd changed her name just as quickly as she'd coloured her mousy brown hair.

Goosebumps raised on her arms as an icy wind tore at her clothes. Morgan stopped a minute to catch her breath, looking out at the verdant fields surrounding her, the battered copse of trees between this sacred place and the bohemian town spread out below it, the endless expanse of countryside that had once been submerged, the Tor an isolated island in the mists of time.

The wind picked up as Morgan renewed her ascent, buffeting against her body, trying to push her off the hill. Sleet struck her cheek as the stormy clouds spilled over into rain. She gritted her teeth and persevered, while her heart lifted at the labour. It was a sign. The fortune teller had told her that the reborn spirit inside her had been cast out of Avalon and that the fae would do everything in their power to keep her away from the portal. Whatever sliver of doubt she may have harboured, the gale swept away.

Planting one foot in front of the other, Morgan forced her way through the wind. Her hair tangled against her face, her hands were cold as ice, her calves were burning from exertion. But the final few steps lay before her. The tower was within reach. She would be home soon.

The wind howled its fury as, gasping for breath, Morgan stumbled through the arch and into the tower.

An eerie silence enveloped her. Morgan stared at the rough stone walls of the tower, blackened with age and slick with moss in places. She slumped down on one of the rocky seats, grateful to be out of the wind's reach. Her eyes steered upwards towards the exposed sky above.

The hair on Morgan's arms stood on end, before a blinding flash of light seared her world white.

She winced as she woke up to a pounding headache. Blinking, her vision slowly blurred into focus. A bed, grey covers, a table at the end with a ledger on it. Bleak, grey walls. A curtain to one side.

She must be in a hospital. Her ears were ringing. Or was that the monitor next to her bed beeping to the tune of her heartbeat?

Her body ached and she winced as she noticed her arms, wrapped in bandages, her hands poking out at the ends, singed red and stinging. She felt heat rise to her cheeks. She'd been a fool.

She turned her head to see her mother asleep in a chair beside her. Two empty coffee cups on the side table meant her father was close, too. They'd come all this way. For her.

Tears welled in her eyes as she swallowed back the lump in her throat. Maybe she'd been mistaken. Maybe she'd been looking in all the wrong places, too preoccupied to see what had always been there.

Yawning, her mother opened her eyes. "Welcome back," she said, a relieved smile wiping years of worry from her worn face.

Maybe it was time to forget about the past.

Maybe she did belong here after all.

DRAGONFALL

A shadow passes overhead and Callum looks up in time to see the dragon plummet from the sky, crashing into a hawthorn thicket not far ahead. For a moment, he stands frozen, memories flashing before his eyes like the scars scrawled across his body. His ears ring with the ghosts of gunfire and he almost tastes the tang of blood in his mouth again as he remembers that last day on the battlefield, alone, the sole survivor of his platoon, trapped underneath the carcass of the beast that had killed them all.

Callum shudders, his hand drifting towards the pistol strapped to his side. Not much use against a dragon, but it wasn't the creature he'd have to fight off this time.

A roar shatters the silence, propelling Callum into action. He drops the rabbit he'd snared for dinner and sprints towards the sound, his boots thumping against the rocky landscape before he passes underneath the canopy of trees. He doesn't care about snapping twigs underfoot or the rustle of underbrush. The beast's thrashing covers any noise he makes.

He slides to a halt when he sees the hunters. There are three of them, armed with rifles and not much more. Amateurs.

Behind them, the dragon rears its wings. One of them has a tear in it, the harpoon still lodged in the membrane between two phalanges scaled in black and amber hues. The beast bellows, a cry filled with both pain and rage. The hunters scatter as the dragon snaps at them, its razor-sharp fangs longer than the guns they carry.

Callum's heart races as the hunters regroup. A round of shots clatters harmlessly off the dragon's scales and one man lunges for the harpoon, the only weapon to hand worth having. If they shred its wing further, the dragon would never fly again. Worse, if they killed it, it could undo everything he'd fought for.

"Hold!" Callum orders, stepping into view, hand resting on his pistol. "You're in violation of the treaty. Drop your weapons and I'll let you live."

Four sets of eyes turn towards him, and Callum tenses as a hunter trains a rifle on him. A sneer pulls the man's grin lopsided. "Mighty confident for someone outnumbered three to one."

Callum shifts his footing, allowing his jacket to fall open, revealing the image tattooed across his bare chest: a stylized dragon gripping a scored shield. His jaw clenches as the hunters' eyes widen in recognition. Even rabble like them know they owe their lives to him.

The hunter licks his lips. "Can't tell anyone if you're dead."

Callum dives sideways as the man pulls the trigger. He rolls and is on his feet in one smooth movement, a shot from his pistol taking the hunter out before the man has a chance to reload. A strangled cry is cut short as the dragon bites the head off the closest hunter, the remains of his corpse dropping to the ground. Callum turns towards the third hunter, his pistol aimed at the man's chest. Wordlessly, the hunter drops his rifle and sinks to his knees, lifting his hands to his head. They shake as Callum kicks the weapon out of the man's reach.

"Go," Callum grunts, and the hunter scrambles to his feet and runs off into the woods.

Callum faces the dragon. The creature eyes him warily, its spiked tail lashing from side to side. The echoes of remembered artillery reverberate to the drumbeat of Callum's heart as the weight of the past presses down on him. So many had died. His eyes sting with the memory of smoke, and blood, and guts, and death.

"You were there," the dragon rumbles, its voice like gravel tumbling down a mountain. In its amber eyes, Callum sees the reflection of his own pain, the fear and regret born from a lifetime of war. They are both survivors. Today and back then.

He holsters his pistol. "Let me take that out." He nods towards the harpoon still stuck in the dragon's wing.

The creature inclines its head and lowers the wing so that Callum can reach easier. Its scales are warm against his skin as Callum gently pries the weapon loose. The tear flaps listlessly in the breeze passing through the woods.

"I can sew it up for you," Callum offers. "I'm no seamstress, but I've enough scars of my own to prove I'm capable."

The dragon lets out a low rumble, a sound that could almost be mistaken for gratitude. Callum returns to the body of the man he had killed and tears a strand of cloth from the man's trousers. He worries the edges until a long thread loosens from the fabric. Then he snaps a thorn off a nearby tree, wraps the thread around it, and carefully begins stitching up the torn wing.

As the needle weaves in and out of the delicate membrane, Callum catches a glimpse of the creature watching him. Its proximity should set the hair at the nape of Callum's neck erect, and yet, he feels no fear. Instead, his heart dances as his fingers work at healing the dragon's injury.

Once he's done, he steps back to let the dragon inspect his handiwork. The beast flaps its wing a few times, testing its strength. Seemingly satisfied, it turns its attention back to Callum.

"Thank you," it says, its eyes filled with gratitude. And then it lifts itself into the air, its wings carrying it effortlessly aloft.

Callum watches the dragon as it flies away, until it is lost in the distance. Somehow, he feels lighter. As if a weight had been lifted from him. The scars of the past are written on his body, but the future is a hope borne on webbed wings.

He may never see that dragon again, but he knows, somehow, that this is not the end.

This is just the beginning.

TWO LONELY HEARTS

I slump back in my chair, exhaling loudly. The evidence of my obsession is spread out on the desk in front of me. Shattered hearts, red paint bleeding on brown bricks, twisting vines and empty frames. Photos taken over the last few months of images I'd stumbled upon in the strangest of places all over the city – behind bakeries, sprawled across abandoned warehouses, on the sides of stationary vehicles. All clearly done by the same graffiti artist.

My fingers linger over my favourite: two lonely figures separated by a storm-drenched chasm. It still moves me in ways I can't explain.

Although, I guess, my recent divorce might have had something to do with it. In fact, it was on my way back to my apartment after signing the papers that I had first spotted this image, tucked away in the alley behind the lawyer's office, where I'd ducked in to get away from the crowds, the overwhelming pressure of a thousand strangers' indifference, to gulp at air that wouldn't fill my gasping lungs as I sank to my knees and wondered how everything had fallen apart so quickly.

And there it was, on the wall in front of me. With the clever stroke of a can of spray paint, someone had perfectly captured my entire existence in shades of red and grey.

As the days went by, I found other images. Or rather, they found me. Always when I was at my lowest, the smell of fresh paint would waft past me, or a stroke of red would catch my eye. Always pictures of a heart broken, of a love lost, of quiet despair. It was as if someone out there could read my mind and was painting it all across the city for others to see.

Frustrated, I gather the pictures into a pile and shove them back into my desk drawer. I have no answers, and I need some fresh air. I grab my coat and step outside, the wet pavement slippery from the recent rain. The odour of rotten refuse hits my nostrils as the sun, hidden behind tall buildings, dips below the horizon, shading the world a dreary monochrome.

I walk, not much caring where I'm going. Somehow, I end up in an alley. An in-between place, the void between a here and a there.

And I am not alone.

The artist steps away from the wall and presses a cap onto the bottle of spray paint she's holding. A paint-spattered hoodie obscures her face, but her presence fills the alley. She lifts her eyes to mine and it is all I can do to keep from losing my mind. A weight of emotions presses down on me, and I grunt underneath the strain. My eyelids flicker uncontrollably as visions assail my mind.

> *A sun-kissed beach, the taste of saltwater on my lips and the wind in my long blonde hair. The soft caress of silk, the warm glow of candlelight, the scent of rose petals strewn across a canopied bed. A husband, uncouth and iron-stained, unloved. A lover, hot-headed warmonger, unfaithful. Countless others, long dead, turned to dust. An eternity of broken promises and broken hearts. Love gained, always lost again and again, over and over again. An ache that can no longer be healed.*

I wrench my gaze from hers and focus on the mural behind her. Butterflies with broken wings, forever trapped within a jar. The style is unmistakable.

"Who are you?" I blurt.

The artist's shoulders slump. "I don't know anymore."

The hoodie slips from her head, revealing a cascade of golden hair. The dying light illuminates a heart-shaped face with lips I suddenly ache to kiss. A bead of sweat runs down my back as my eyes follow the contours of her body. Perfection. A goddess born to be worshipped.

Understanding dawns. My eyes snap back to hers. "You're…" I swallow, my throat suddenly dry. Her name caresses my lips. Aphrodite.

"The goddess of love?" she sneers, turning her back on me. She rips the cap from the can of spray paint, studies the wall again. "I believed in love once. I was mistaken."

The smell of ozone and paint reaches my nostrils. Thunder rumbles in the distance. She sprays bold strokes against the brick, angry red slashes like open wounds and unhealed scars.

But I've had time to think since that day I first stumbled upon her work. I lick my lips, and then say the words I should have said to myself, so many months ago.

"You are more than their love. You are enough, just as you are."

Her hands still, her body suddenly taut with tension.

Lightning flashes overhead. I look up at the sky just as rain starts pouring down. I turn back to the artist. She's gone.

Wet paint runs down the wall, the severe strokes softened into something smoother, undefined.

The sun sparkles down from a cloudless sky and

the subtle scent of roses envelopes me as I take a seat on a park bench. Birdsong and the sounds of children playing on the soft grass fill the air. Couples holding hands walk past, eyes only for each other. I don't envy them. Their happiness no longer threatens my own.

A stroke of red on the dustbin closest to me catches my eye. Curious, I get up again to investigate.

My breath hitches in my throat. It's one of hers. But different.

A phoenix rising from the ashes.

The dustbin rattles as a can of spray paint is tossed into it. I lift my gaze and see her studying me. Her golden hair glows in the sunlight as an easy smile flits across her face.

For a moment, we stare at each other – two strangers who once shared broken hearts. But only memories of those old wounds remain now. Dulled by time, faded into wisdom.

I return the smile and she laughs before turning around and sauntering away.

The sun kisses my skin as I take my seat on the park bench again. Inhaling deeply, I sigh blissfully. It really is a beautiful day.

GRAVE CORRESPONDENCE

I am sitting at my desk, answering notes of commiseration, when a tapping sound startles me so my quill scrawls across the paper, leaving a large black stain that smudges my empty words into illegibility. Tutting, I turn towards the window. My breath hitches into my throat at the sight of a large black crow on the windowsill, eyeing me intently. In its beak, it holds a rumpled letter.

I consider calling for my guard, but the bird's beak taps against the windowpane again, impatiently, and I rise slowly, hesitantly. Its beady eyes watch me as I walk over, encumbered by heavy mourning skirts, and fling the window open.

The crow squawks as it flaps into the air and I duck as it takes a turn around my room, drops the letter onto my desk, and then departs again, its ebony wings glinting in the moonlight. I risk a glance outside, but spy nothing but empty grounds around the keep's wall. Whoever had sent the bird is long gone.

Closing the window again, I gravitate towards the missive. It, too, is stained, but with scattered drops of burgundy. My hands shake as my eyes rove across the scrawling words.

> *The poison was slow to act, but potent, as you must have known it would be. Your husband suspected nothing, and in the end, death came swiftly. The healer saw nothing but the king's weak heart, perhaps enfeebled by the many*

*uncertainties of a war waged too long. You covered
your tracks well.*

But I know the truth, now.

Gasping, I toss the letter into the crackling flames of the hearth, my heart thumping against my chest as I watch it shrivel and turn to ashes. Fear slithers icily down my spine.

No one must know. On this all depends.

❧❖❧

Days pass in an agony of uncertainty. I jump at every loud noise; every lingering look is a vice around my heart. And still, no one comes forward to accuse me. I discard mourning black for robes of pure white threaded with royal gold. My nerves settle. I dare to believe the threat averted.

But then, on the night of my coronation, another knock upon my window disturbs my peace. Once more, the shadowy messenger flaps into my room, carrying a missive in its beak. The crow's unblinking gaze leaves me paralysed as it deposits the paper upon my desk. It screeches loudly, turning my blood to ice, and departs again on shadowy wings.

A foul stench assaults my nose as I edge closer, as if the paper had been dipped in carrion filth. The words scribbled on it were filled with vitriol.

*Woman, you go too far! Perhaps your crime could
be excused if it had been a matter of the heart,
but your husband's place is taken by no suitor.
The king is dead, and now you sit on his throne.
Power-hungry harpy!*

*This kingdom, already so ravaged, will burn for
your heartless ambition.*

The letter crumples in my hand. Angrily, I toss it into the fire. What I had done, I did not for me but for the good of the kingdom. Whoever this mysterious correspondent may be, he has no right to judge my actions. I shall proceed as intended and trust the outcome of events to vouch for me.

Months pass in a flurry of activity as I negotiate treaties, broker peaceful agreements, harbour the destitute, and begin making amends for the wrongs my husband had caused. Our neighbours, once staunchly united against us, send tokens of their restored regard. Under new laws and aided by trade agreements that will, in time, ensure hitherto unseen economic success, our kingdom begins to flourish once again.

I have all but forgotten the previous missives, but when the crow raps upon my window once more, whatever burdens of conscience I might have carried before had long since been discarded. I open the window and watch as it takes its usual route around my room, silent as a ghost this time. It lands upon my desk, dropping the letter as it does so, and takes a moment to preen its jet-black feathers. I venture a glance out the window. Apart from shadows cast by the full moon, there is nothing to see. The bird's sender still eludes me.

A breath of wind caresses my face as the crow flaps past me, out the window, and disappears into the night.

What accusations await me this time? I cross the room and pick up the folded piece of paper, rough against my fingertips, like gravel on a grave. A gasp escapes my lips as I read the words.

Dearest queen, you are a better ruler than I ever

was.

Your husband rests in peace now.

Darkness envelops me as the letter falls from my hand.

❧ ◆ ❧

Years have passed since that night and although I have seen many crows since, none of them have come bearing messages from the beyond again. The wars that had nearly destroyed us are long since forgotten and our kingdom thrives. It will soon be time to hand the burden of rule on to a worthy successor.

I hope that, when the time comes and, should circumstance demand it, the winged messenger will carry my missives too, as it once did for my departed husband.

RETURN TO AVALON

G ale force winds whipped past the tower on top of Glastonbury Tor. Morgan pulled her black leather jacket close about herself as she stood just outside the doorway, hesitating. She glanced down at her hands, where barely healed burn scars laid testimony to her last ascent.

Could she risk entering the tower again?

She looked up at the clear blue sky. No clouds, and no chance of lightning this time.

Morgan gritted her teeth and crossed the threshold.

A blinding flash of light seared her world white, and Morgan winced, bracing for pain. "Not again," she muttered, wondering what one person's odds were of being struck twice in a lifetime.

But no pain came.

As the glare faded, Morgan's eyes widened. She was in an apple orchard. The sounds of twittering birds filled the air, heavy with the scent of summer blossoms. A bee buzzed past her and Morgan's gaze followed it until she saw a meadow beyond the trees with a pavilion standing in the verdant grass, colourful pennons flapping in the gentle breeze.

Bemused, she wandered towards the tent, stopping to pluck a ruby apple from a tree. She bit into it and gasped as she felt all weariness wash from her. Amazed, she watched the scars fade from her hands until nothing but smooth skin remained.

"Avalon," she whispered breathlessly as her hands started to tremble. "I'm... home."

She dropped the apple and ran towards the pavilion. She burst through the door flap and stopped short as three faces turned towards her. They were young like her, and dressed in jeans and sneakers; two guys and a girl.

"Ugh, what is she doing here?" the girl exclaimed, rolling her eyes. She was pretty, in a conventional way: blonde hair, blue eyes, legs that went on for miles.

"Who are you, then?" one guy asked. His dark hair hung in artful locks around shoulders so shapely that Morgan suspected he spent hours looking at them in a gym. He frowned at her like she was a puzzle, not to be solved, but to be cracked.

"Isn't it obvious?" the second guy said. Morgan shuffled self-consciously as he stared at her with his intense green eyes. He raked a hand through his coppery hair and said: "She's my sister."

"Sister!" Morgan exclaimed, echoed by the dark-haired guy. The girl grimaced and clenched her manicured hands into fists. "What do you mean, sister?" Morgan asked as a thousand moths fluttered inside her chest.

The redhead laughed. "Okay, half-sister! Or so the legends say, at least. You *are* her, aren't you? Morganna?"

"Morgan," she murmured, feeling slightly faint.

"Sure," the guy said easily. "And I'm Art. This is Lance," he said, nodding at the dark-haired guy, who looked just as shocked as Morgan felt. "And the lovely lady over there is Gwen."

"Ah, I see you've all arrived. Splendid!"

Morgan spun around as a man strode into the tent. Countless hours spent poring over old texts, reading every bit of legend and lore she could get her hands on, had not prepared her for coming face to face with a man stepped straight out of myth. He was wearing a dark blue loose-fitting robe and held a twisted wooden staff in one hand. A close-cropped grey beard framed a face strangely unlined by time, but his eyes carried the weight of ages.

"Merlin!" Gwen gasped, and the old man nodded at her. Morgan wrapped her arms around herself and tried to fade into the background as the guys stepped forward to greet the old man. Art shook his hand vehemently, while Lance bobbed beside him, seeming giddy with excitement.

"It's really true then, isn't it?" Gwen asked as she hugged the old man. "We *are* the legends reborn?"

Morgan's breath hitched in her throat. All these years, all this time... she had *hoped*. But had she really ever believed?

Merlin's gaze swept towards Morgan, and she lifted her chin, forcing herself to meet his eyes. She clenched her fists and reminded herself that she had nothing to be ashamed of. The old stories revered demure women and reviled those with power. If she really was Morganna la Fay reborn, then Morgan promised herself she would live up to her name.

"It's true," Merlin said. "And happy as I am to see you all again, I'm afraid your coming heralds a great doom."

Morgan watched the others as Merlin spoke. Art was frowning, Lance was leaning forward eagerly, and Gwen's eyes were wide with alarm. Her own chest felt like it was about to burst and she let out a soft breath, feeling the tension ease in her shoulders.

"Excalibur has been taken," Merlin continued grimly. "And if it is not returned soon, the magic of Avalon will fade and a grey darkness will steal over all the lands until there is no hope left in the world, neither in the realms of the fae nor in those of man."

Lance's grin split his handsome face. "Who took it? Just point me at them. I will have the sword back in no time."

"We," Art added, and the two guys high-fived each other while Gwen batted her eyelashes at both of them.

Morgan rolled her eyes.

"I applaud your enthusiasm," Merlin said, and Morgan noticed the corners of his mouth twitching with amusement. "But it will not be as simple as you think. The lady Nimue is formidable…" His voice faltered and his eyes lost focus for a moment. Then he shook himself and continued. "You will need to unlock the powers of your past selves to overcome the challenges she will set before you can face her and reclaim Excalibur. Are you up to the task?"

"Hell yes!" the guys shouted. Gwen seemed less eager, but she nodded, before all eyes turned to Morgan.

A surge of warmth radiated throughout her body. Finally.

"Teach me," she said, her heart drumming in her chest.

WHISPERS OF WAR

They used to shout your name, long ago. The sound echoed off the walls of fortress cities gleaming underneath a temperate sun, mingling with the breeze as it thrummed through canyons where lush grass swayed and livestock multiplied, and vibrated on the shields and spears of the people of Zalara as they fought for your glory.

Mavuto, the warrior god, protector of the brave.

The people praised your name as you guided their kingdom to power and riches. You were their patron god of victory; they laid their success at your feet as small tribes united into a kingdom as far-reaching as the stars spanning the nighttime sky. It was a time of prosperity, where water ran freely and no man went hungry. The people of Zalara were satisfied. They hung up their spears and, for a time, there was peace.

But peace did not suit you, Mavuto.

You craved the smell of blood shed on battlefields, smoke rising heavenwards as homes burned, the anguished calls of the defeated. You spurred their leaders on until Zalara wanted more than was their due. Dignity vanished from their eyes, replaced by a cold, ruthless hunger. Greed turned to corruption. Arrogance sparked the flames of discontent and soon war was brewing again.

Once more, your name was on their lips, Mavuto.

But something had changed. Where war had once been honourable, fought by the brave for the betterment of all, now it turned into vicious conquest. Zalara craved more, and they took it with force. The echoes of clashing swords and thunderous battle cries echoed through the canyons as violence shattered the kingdom's tranquillity. Innocents were slaughtered, blood flowed as freely as water once had, and the survivors suffered under the yoke of merciless tyrants. The acrid smell of smoke hung heavy in the air as the land dried up and the livestock died. The mournful wails of grieving mothers pierced the night while children cried themselves to sleep, hungry and homeless. As the horrors of war grew, the people became desperate.

It could not last, Mavuto.

Dust now swirls around the ruins of your broken temples and the remnants of the once-great kingdom of Zalara. Its people took up their spears and turned them against their leaders. They shrugged off the shackles of oppression, broke the bonds that countless battles had forged, and fled with their families, scattering with the wind. Haunted by nightmares of the past, the people renounced their power-hungry patron.

Your name, Mavuto, was whispered in fear and regret, until it was all but forgotten.

For centuries, the scorching sun beat down relentlessly, blistering the sand beneath its fiery gaze, ravaging the land and the people as if punishing them for past sins. Where lush grass once danced in the gentle breeze, barren wastelands now stretched as far as the eye could see. The once majestic fortress walls disappeared as, little by little, their stones were carried away to build makeshift shelters, and sweltering sands swept the last traces of Zalara away, lost forever. Hardened by suffering, the people now eke out a meagre living, and they murmur around campfires, telling stories that were memories long ago.

They used to shout your name, Mavuto. Now they whisper it.

They whisper tales of a warrior god who led his people to power. Of a land that brimmed with water and food, where green grass wafted in a cool breeze, and where the mighty took what they wanted and victory was the spoils of the strongest. Their whispers, once filled with fear and regret, now kindle anticipation and unrest. They beat their spears against their shields as they invoke your name again, god of war. The sands are shifting. The people are restless once more.

They whisper your name now, Mavuto. Soon they will shout it again.

GUARDIAN OF TRUTH

The market seemed busier than usual. It buzzed with an energy that was almost frenetic as Azim wove through the labyrinth of narrow alleys and crowded stalls, jostling elbows with tourists and locals alike. His nimble fingers dipped into pockets undetected while their owners haggled with vendors over vibrant textiles, intricate brass lamps, and delicate silver jewellery.

The air was thick with the scent of spices and the aroma of freshly baked bread, and Azim's stomach rumbled as his nose caught a whiff of kebabs rotating on a spit at a nearby hole-in-the-wall. Pausing in the shade of a towering minaret, Azim inspected the morning's takings.

His shoulders slumped as the bitter taste of disappointment flooded his mouth. Small change. Hardly enough for breakfast, and not enough to get him out of the back alleys of Cairo any time soon.

He was going to have to set his sights higher, Azim realised as his eyes roved across the surrounding stalls. His gaze landed on a small shop he had never seen open before. Today, it was so crowded by the press of bodies that he couldn't see what was on offer.

Azim pushed closer until he reached the front of the crowd. His eyes widened. The walls of the shop were lined with shelves stacked with ancient relics – statues of the old gods, papyrus scrolls, amulets and gold rings, gold-lacquered furniture, heavy stone slabs covered in pictograms, and countless other smaller trinkets. The treasures filled the small space so there was barely enough room for the two men inside. Azim strained to hear what they were saying, but they kept their voices low and their hand gestures small.

A glimmer caught the corner of Azim's vision, and his gaze was drawn to a relic shaped into a stylised eye. A rich, deep-blue lapis lazuli inlay formed the iris, surrounded by delicate lines of red carnelian and green malachite markings, almost like the sun's expanding rays, and encased within a polished gold frame intricately engraved with hieroglyphics. It fit perfectly into the palm of his hand as his fingers wrapped around it.

"You! Boy! Drop that relic!"

The shop owner glared at him, and Azim had just enough time to see the scar running across the other man's eye as he turned around before adrenaline kicked in. He shot through the door and pushed past the bystanders, ignoring their protests and slipping through hands reaching to grab him, and sprinted down the alley.

The sound of pursuit followed him. Azim swerved past people as he ran through the maze of passageways, vaulting across baskets filled with dates, ducking underneath hanging carpets, avoiding a camel calmly chewing on a piece of cloth next to a fabric stall, and finally sprinting into a small, secluded courtyard. A stack of crates stood to one side, and a few half-empty boxes of spices rested on an abandoned cart. Azim's breath was ragged as he searched for a way out, but he was trapped.

He spun around just as the scarred man stepped into view, blocking his only exit. A sneer pulled one corner of the man's mouth upward as he held his hand out to Azim.

"Give me the Eye of Ra, boy, and no harm will come to you."

An icy feeling washed across Azim, and he shook

his head as a sense of wrongness flooded his entire body. The man was lying. Azim didn't know how he knew that, but he knew it for certain.

"Why should I believe you, Scarface?" Azim snapped, retreating a few steps.

The man looked startled for a moment, his hand darting towards his eye before he recovered. A look of wonder crept across his face. "You can see this?" he asked. "So, it is true then…" He clenched his hand into a fist. "Give me that relic!"

"No." Azim's back was to a wall. He was running out of options. "Finder's keepers. If you want it, you'll have to pay me for it."

"Fine," the man said, and Azim blinked, surprised. "Name your price."

Azim frowned. It shouldn't be this easy. He looked at the relic, still clasped firmly in his hand. Clearly, this was not some ordinary trinket. As he stared into the iris, it almost seemed as if the eye had some inner glow. As if someone was looking back.

"You don't know what you're dealing with, boy," the man warned, his voice low with threat. "The Eye of Ra is not to be trifled with. I am not to be trifled with."

A warmth flushed through Azim's body. Scarface was telling the truth. Azim shook his head again, trying to clear his thoughts. How could he be so sure? Was it the relic?

"What is this thing?" he mumbled to himself.

To his surprise, Scarface replied. "It is the Eye of Ra, imbued with the powers of the Sun God himself. It allows one to see through illusions and lies." Heat rushed through Azim's body as the man talked. "I belong to the Order of Ma'at. It is our sacred duty to bring truth and balance to the world. Name your price and the Order will pay it."

Azim's breath hitched in his throat. This was it. This was his way out of here. He said a number, something so ridiculous he almost laughed at himself.

Scarface simply nodded. "Agreed. Now hand over the Eye."

Almost giddy with excitement, Azim took a step closer, holding the relic out. He could hardly believe his luck. "And you'll use this for good?"

"Of course," Scarface retorted irritably, reaching for the Eye.

An icy cold flush doused the smile from Azim's lips. His entire body shook with the untruth of those two words.

He reacted instinctively. His other hand shot out, grabbing a fistful of the red spice in the abandoned cart and throwing it into Scarface's eyes. As the man bellowed in pain, Azim leaped onto the stacked crates and scrambled onto the roof.

He ran. He ran until his lungs screamed and his sides ached and his breath came in big gulps. Finally, when he couldn't take another step, he ducked into the gap of a boarded-up window in an abandoned building, and lay there, gasping for breath, until he was sure he hadn't been followed.

When the sky turned orange, Azim finally emerged from his hiding place and found a quiet spot on a rooftop from where he could see the city spread out beneath him. He had spent his entire life in those alleys, dodging trouble as he scraped by, just trying to survive. And there were countless others like him down there.

He gripped the Eye of Ra in his hand. Azim knew the Order of Ma'at would be looking for him, and he also knew that he could not let the relic fall into their hands. Scarface had spoken of truth and balance, but the Eye had seen through his deception. He would use the relic to manipulate and enforce his version of order, no matter the cost.

If the Eye fell into the wrong hands, how many lives would be at risk?

Azim nodded to himself. He would be its

guardian now. He would use the Eye of Ra to protect his city and make a better life for others like him. This was his chance to make a difference. He would ensure the truth was wielded for the right reasons.

It was not the escape he had wanted, but he knew it was the right thing to do.

And Azim's body burned with the truth of it.

DANCE OF THE LOST SOULS

I peer out from behind the elaborate mask, gaping at the palazzos on either side of the canal. The only sound I can hear is the slapping of oars as my gondolier skilfully manoeuvres his little boat underneath a stone bridge. Fog hangs low over the surrounding buildings, bringing with it the scent of the lagoon and casting the yellowish lights of sporadic lanterns into eerie shadows.

My gloved hand slides across the silk of my borrowed black gown and I have to pinch myself to make sure I'm not dreaming. I can hardly believe I'm here, in Venice, and on my way to a mysterious masked ball. *'Come, if you dare'* the card had said, slipped underneath the door of my hotel room. I'd thought it a prank until the receptionist's envious glare had proved me wrong.

"You must go," she insisted with a smile that hadn't reached her eyes. "I've only heard rumours about this ball. It's very exclusive. You are fortunate to have been invited. But you must wear a mask."

"I have one," I said, smiling, as I remembered the beautiful souvenir I had acquired earlier that morning.

I'd spent days perusing the wares of stalls around the Ponte di Rialto, never satisfied until I'd ventured into the smaller alleys, letting myself get lost, and finally stumbled upon a craftsman's shop so tucked away I might have missed it had the mask in the window not caught my eye. My fingers had brushed reverently across it when the man took it down, sure I could never afford it. The face was made from the palest porcelain, the black Burano lace as delicate as a spider's web, and the red lips painted with a smile as mysterious as the Mona Lisa's.

"How much?" I'd asked, prepared for disappointment.

Instead of answering, the man had studied me for a moment, his eyes carefully considering me. "Why are you here?" he asked, his Italian accent sharp as an espresso.

"I'm on holiday." I shrugged, carefully avoiding his gaze.

"And?"

The word lingered in the air between us.

I swallowed as my anxiety tried to overwhelm me. I thought of the life I had left behind, the one I would have to return to in a few days. The one that was so *ordinary*, so boring, that the mere thought of it threatened to bring tears to my eyes. I wanted more. I wanted to escape.

I don't know how much of that he had read in my evasive eyes, but he nodded to himself and said: "It's yours." I protested, but he insisted. "It is mine to give away," he said gently. "And I want you to have it, *signorina.*"

My breath hitches in my throat as the gondola turns a corner and the winged lions of Piazza San Marco appear out of the mist, like two stone guardians standing watch on their tall plinths. Deftly, the gondolier steers the boat to the edge of the plain before offering a hand to help me out. The heels of my lace-up boots clack on the stone tiles as I disembark.

St Mark's Campanile looms over me while the darkened windows of the Doge's Palace stare blindly down, empty sockets above a gaping mouth. Through the fog, I can barely make out the curves of the domed roof of Saint Mark's Basilica.

The plain is empty.

Disappointment weighs down my shoulders. I

must have the date wrong.

I turn around. The gondola is gone.

Strands of my long black hair tickle across my face as a soft breeze brushes my body. *"Come,"* a voice whispers in my ear as the hair on my arms lifts.

Slowly, I turn back toward the piazza. It's no longer deserted.

Masked figures fill the plain, all dressed in black like I am, moving in groups of two to the steps of a dance murmuring through the air. Their movements are as ethereal as the soft lights flickering through the fog.

Mesmerised, I move closer. My feet carry me into the dance of their own accord until I find myself in the centre of the group. A masked man takes my hand and leads me through the steps. I twirl and glide, giddy with the sheer joy of the movement, the spectacle, the mystery of it all.

We dance and dance until I am breathless and my feet ache, and still we dance. I can feel the music in my bones. It never stops, and it carries me with it.

Gasping for breath, I try to pull away from my partner, but he grips my hand tighter. I lose my balance and step into another couple's path. An icy shiver runs down my spine as they pass right through me.

My heartbeat drowns out the music as I see the dancers for what they really are: ghosts trapped in an eternal dance, their movements graceful, yet haunting. Somehow, I've stumbled into something definitely not *ordinary*. My breath becomes ragged as panic rises within me. I try to scream, but no sound escapes my lips. It's as if I have become a ghost myself, imprisoned in this eerie dance of the afterlife.

My partner's grip on my hand is unyielding, the eyes peeking out from behind his mask stern. I take a deep breath, willing my heart rate to slow. The tension in my shoulders dissipates as I let the music wash over me again.

Satisfied, my partner bows elegantly, and I return a graceful curtsy. I clear my mind and forget about my fears, and let him sweep me off into the eternal dance once more.

Prefer your endings to be happy? Follow the link below to read this story with an alternative ending.

SUNEELEROUX.COM/DANCE-OF-THE-LOST-SOULS-HAPPY-ENDING/

CRISPIN'S CHRISTMAS QUEST

O ne Christmas Eve not too long ago, old Mrs Clauson pulled a tray out of the oven and sighed contentedly as the scent of cinnamon and cloves filled her little bakery. Carefully, she placed the gingerbread man on a cooling tray and, after it had cooled down and with hands steady despite her advanced years, she piped delicate lace cuffs, a snowy collar, and a frilled beanie. Last, she added two gumdrop eyes and a red U-shaped mouth.

Mrs Clauson stood back and inspected her handiwork. It made her smile.

And so, as a wishing star shot past the window outside, she named the gingerbread man Crispin and gave him pride of place on the shelf behind the till – not to be sold, but to bring joy to everyone who entered her shop, a gentle reminder of the spirit of the season.

Had Mrs Clauson lingered much longer, she would have seen that Christmas miracles were indeed real, but instead she went to bed, satisfied with the night's work. Wrapped up snugly in her goose down comforter, Mrs Clauson didn't see the gumdrop eyes blink or the little red mouth forming a surprised oh as Crispin, the gingerbread man, stretched to life and surveyed his surroundings.

His sugary eyes darted from the beautifully-decorated fir tree in the corner to the red-and-green bunting hanging from wood-panelled ceilings, to the shelves lined with mouthwatering cakes and creams, and finally landed on the batch of star-frost cookies

Mrs Clauson had left on the counter, ready for the villagers who would visit her in the morning, looking for something special to mark the occasion. Born of enchantment, Crispin immediately sensed the magic in those sweet treats: infused with love, they would bring goodwill and happiness to all who tasted them.

A shiver fluttered across the gingerbread man's body as the window suddenly creaked open. Crispin's eyes widened as an elf snuck into the shop. The creature's pointy ears drooped below a ragged hat that had once been striped in white and red but was now covered in dirt. His boots were spattered with muddy slush and his tunic was missing at least two silver buttons. The elf cackled greedily as he darted towards the counter and started piling star-frost cookies into a tattered bag.

"Hey," Crispin said in a voice coated with sugar. "Who are you?"

Startled, the elf glanced around until his gaze landed on the gingerbread man. "They're all mine!" he sneered, before darting towards the window and leaping out of the shop.

"Wait!" shouted Crispin, but it was too late. Of Mrs Clauson's special cookies, only a few crumbs remained on the counter.

Sadness overwhelmed the gingerbread man as he imagined the old baker's face the next morning when she realised her special treats had been stolen. He thought of the villagers' disappointment, and of how Christmas would be ruined if he didn't get those cookies back.

And so Crispin jumped off the shelf and clambered out the window. He marvelled at the snowflakes falling like magical stars from the sky, and at how they clung to his gingerbread body for a moment like a thousand tiny hugs, until he realised they had obscured any footprints the elf might have left. But the magic of the cookies lingered in the air.

Crispin followed its trail. Past houses gleaming

with frost and Christmas lights, beyond the borders of the little village and out into the dark woods. Had the gingerbread man known about the dangers of the forest, of sharp-toothed wolves and snowy owls hunting on ghostly wings, he might have turned back to the safety of the bakery. But he didn't, and so he followed the magical trail to a hollow tree where he found the elf sobbing, an untasted cookie in one hand.

"What's the matter?" Crispin asked quietly, his red mouth turned down sadly.

"I'm a bad elf!" the little thief wailed. "I shouldn't have stolen these cookies, and I shouldn't have burned last year's batch!" Tears rolled down his cheeks and plopped wetly on the mossy ground.

With compassion born of the hopes and dreams carried on the wishing star whose powers infused him, Crispin put his arm around the elf. "You can't change your yesterday, but you can change your tomorrow."

The elf blinked. He stared at the gingerbread man for a moment. And then he nodded. "Let's take these back," he said, as he placed the cookie he had been holding back into the bag.

Together, the elf and the gingerbread man made their way back to town. The sun was just peeking out from behind snow-capped mountains, setting the frost-covered ground to sparkling, when they climbed through the window and into the welcoming warmth of the bakery.

Mrs Clauson stood next to the empty plate, looking sad and forlorn. She turned as an icy breeze wafted from the window. "Crispin!" she gasped as she saw the gingerbread man, and then her eyes widened in surprise. "And Tinsel!"

The elf cleared his throat, holding the bag out at the baker. "I'm sorry, Mistress. I'm a bad elf."

"You're no such thing!" Mrs Clauson dropped to her knees and enveloped the elf in a warm hug. "I've missed you so, this past year. Why did you leave?"

A flush crept across Tinsel's cheeks. "I... I.." he stammered. "I burned the star-frost cookies. I thought you'd be mad."

Mrs Clauson shook her head. "Mistakes happen," she said, tears in her eyes. "I made another batch after you'd gone, but they were not as good as always." She climbed to her feet, reached behind the counter, and pulled out a small apron. "Please stay."

A grin split the elf's face as he accepted the apron. "I'll put these back in their place," he said, pulling a cookie from his tattered bag.

Mrs Clauson turned to Crispin. "Thank you for bringing my friend back. I hope you'll stay too?"

The gingerbread man nodded, and Mrs Clauson lifted him up and returned him to his place on the shelf, from where he watched contentedly as the baker opened the door for the first customer to come in search of a special Christmas treat.

ACKNOWLEDGEMENTS

Somehow I manage to write a weird little story every month and - beyond all expectations - people seem to enjoy them! Thank you to everyone who has ever taken the time to read my sparks of inspiration and written an email to tell me they liked them! You keep me motivated and your e-mails make my day!

As always, a special thank you to Schalk van der Merwe for cheering me on and brainstorming with me. You make my writing life more fun, buddy!

Last but not least, thank you to my hubby, Gareth, for always being there when I need you, and for making my mundane life a little more magical every day.

WANT MORE?

For more titles in the Reverie Flash Fiction series:

SUNEELEROUX.COM/BOOKS/REVERIE-FLASH-FICTION/

If you've enjoyed this book, please consider leaving a review on Goodreads or your platform of choice.

ABOUT THE AUTHOR

Suneé le Roux is a South African author of contemporary and high fantasy stories that blend myth, magic, and adventure. She lives in South Africa with her Welsh husband and their young wizard-in-training.

She loves nothing more than to hear from readers. Connect with her here:

Website: www.suneeleroux.com

Email: contact@suneeleroux.com

Facebook: www.facebook.com/
authorsuneeleroux/

Instagram: www.instagram.com/suneeleroux/

WWW.SUNEELEROUX.COM

Read on for an extract from

MYTH
HUNTER
(MYTHICAL MENAGERIE SERIES #1)

Beginner's Luck

"Shit!" I swore as I stumbled and fell flat on my face.

I lay there for a few seconds, contemplating life, love, the universe and everything else, all the while getting soaked to the bone by the incessant drizzle that had turned the streets of London into a slippery nightmare. It took me a while to realise that both my hands, currently stretched out before me as if in supplication to some uncaring, yet doubtlessly chortling, deity, were touching bits of paper. I clutched onto them as I pushed myself to my feet, ignoring the stares of passersby, none of whom had even the slightest decency to offer a hand.

In my right hand was some kind of wanted advert. I scrunched it up and pushed it into the pocket of my tweed jacket.

Of more interest was what I held in my left hand. A fifty-pound note! I stared at it dumbly, numbly, not believing my luck. A stupid smile crept across my face. I got to eat steak tonight!

That smile twisted into a scowl when I saw the reason for my fall. The sole on the right foot of my best pair of loafers gaped wide open. My sock was sticking out. Not exactly the impression I wanted to make at tomorrow's interview. Not that it would make any difference, I imagine. I could show up in a suit made of hundred-pound notes and I would still not get the job. The financial world was unforgiving, especially if you'd made the sort of mistake I had made.

Still, I had to try. Giving up meant not eating, and forfeiting on this month's rent. And, worst of all, having to listen to yet another one of Mother's tirades.

I surveyed my surroundings, trying to get my bearings again while absentmindedly scratching my stubbly chin. I had just crossed Westminster Bridge on my way home from an interview in the South Bank. Big Ben towered over me, like some giant from myth; silent, judgmental, implacable. Both tourists and Londoners swarmed past me, indifferent to just one more well-dressed twenty-something hoping to somehow survive in this pitiless city.

I squinted as a trickle of water dribbled from my sandy blond hair into my eyes. A rainbow arched over the Houses of Parliament and descended towards the Tube station where the sign for a shoe repair shop caught my eye. I pulled my jacket closer about myself and hurried towards it.

A bell jingled as I walked through the door, the strong odour of shoe polish and sweaty feet assaulting my nose. A man slightly older than me looked up from behind the counter where he was busy repairing someone's footwear. His red hair blazed like a furnace in the darkness of the tiny, windowless shop, reflecting the light from a single spotlight that provided just enough illumination for him to work by. An easy smile crossed his freckled face, blue eyes twinkling with merriment as he greeted me with a distinct Irish lilt.

"What can I do for you?"

I pointed at my offending shoe. "Think you can

fix this?"

The man held out his hand and I passed him the shoe, feeling ridiculous standing there in my slightly soggy sock. He stroked his short-cropped beard thoughtfully as he inspected the grinning sole. "Expensive brand," he noted. "You really should take better care of these."

"Can you save it?" I asked, knowing full well I couldn't afford to replace it.

"Sure," the redhead said. "Ten pounds. Come back tomorrow."

"Tomorrow? You want me to walk home barefoot in the rain?" I asked, looking pointedly towards the door where the inlaid glass had steamed up, obscuring the view outside.

The man shrugged.

"Look," I said. "I need that shoe. Is there any way you can fix it now?"

"Sorry, mate," he replied, nodding at the pile of shoes lying on the countertop already. "Got a bit of a backlog here. But..." He reached below the counter and pulled out a pair of white trainers with a green four-leaved clover embellishment adorning the sides.

"My own design," the shoemaker said proudly.

"How much?" I asked. Unfortunately, the days where I refused to wear anything that wasn't a high street brand were long gone.

"Twenty quid."

I sighed. Those fifty pounds were dwindling fast. I handed the note over and sat down to try the trainers on.

"What name should I put on your slip?" the man asked as I tied the shoelaces.

"Ambrose Davids."

"That's... unusual," he said diplomatically.

"You can thank my mother for that," I replied, taking a few steps in my new trainers. They did fit remarkably well. Not particularly stylish, and paired with my brown tweed suit downright ridiculous, but they would have to do for now.

He handed me my change and the slip.

"Thanks," I said in way of farewell. I opened the door and stepped out of his shop.

Thankfully, the rain had stopped, replaced by a bitingly icy wind. I thrust my hands into my pockets and remembered the other piece of paper I had picked up earlier as my fingers brushed across it. I pulled it out and stared at it.

Instead of the wanted ad I had first assumed, it was a flyer promoting an information session for jobseekers. No further details, just the location, date and time. I looked at my watch and swore again. The session was in fifteen minutes, and about a mile from here. Heedless of the stares once again directed my way, I set out at a jog.

The easiest route was through St James' Park. Ducks quacked as I ran past, dodging pedestrians and cyclists alike. I was out of breath by the time I sprinted past the old war memorial on Waterloo and dripping with sweat when I finally reached Piccadilly Circus, barely sparing a glance for the statue of Anteros and the crowd of camera-wielding tourists around it. By the time I found the unobtrusive door of the venue hidden in a side street, I was already ten minutes late.

The door clicked open when I pressed the buzzer, revealing an empty landing area and a narrow staircase. I took the stairs up two at a time and entered a darkened room on the second floor where a dozen or so people were already watching a slide show. I sat down in the back row, waving apologetically at the presenter in the front as she continued talking.

The woman looked to be in her early twenties too, with dark chocolate skin and a waterfall of black curls framing her face. Her accent was as English as my own, but the African-print scarf wrapped around her throat hinted at a more exotic background.

"As you can see," she was saying, "we are interested in creatures of a more... shall we say, unusual... reputation." She pointed at the screen where a picture of a winged horse on an old Grecian vase was displayed. "We specialise in animals of myth, folklore and fantasy. Your job would be to locate and acquire these creatures on our behalf. This does not come without an element of danger, but you will be handsomely compensated for any risks you may need to take. All we ask is that you deliver the creatures into our care alive and unharmed. Any questions?"

"Yeah." The guy in front of me raised his hand. "What have you been smoking, lady?"

I glanced at the faces around me as laughter bubbled throughout the room. Almost everyone looked sceptical, some shaking their heads in amusement, others frowning in annoyance. One or two even glanced at their watches, barely bothering to hide their yawns.

"I assure you, we are not crazy. These creatures may be scarce, but they are as real as you and I." The presenter looked calmly at the sea of disbelieving faces staring at her. "And they are in danger. They need to be protected."

The man scoffed again, turning an incredulous gaze at the surrounding people. "Is she serious?" he asked of the room. He picked up his coat and stood up. "I'm out of here, lady. Thanks for the fairy tale, but I have mouths to feed. I wouldn't want to send my children off to find the gingerbread house in the woods." More laughter followed as he strode out of the room. One by one, the rest of the people stood up and left, too.

"What a waste of time," a woman said to her friend as they shuffled past me.

The presenter made no move to stop them, but her shoulders slumped a little as she bent over her laptop and turned the presentation off. She flicked a switch on the wall, bathing the room in fluorescent light. Her eyes widened when she saw me still sitting in my chair.

"Was there something?" she asked, a small frown creasing her forehead.

I stood up, not sure how to explain to her I was desperate enough to go in search of fairy tales if it meant I could eat something other than dry bread the rest of this week. Hell, for a small stipend I would swim the length of the Thames in search of selkies or whatever imaginary creature they wanted right now, no matter if I ended up on Sky News tonight.

"Well, uh..." I hesitated as her brown eyes met my own. She looked me over with one eyebrow raised quizzically. I must look a mess, I realised, all sweaty from the jog here and wearing a water-stained suit. I ran a hand self-consciously through my windblown hair.

"I like your shoes," she said, a small smile playing across her lips. She held her right hand out and I shook it automatically. "Amari Kerubo of the CPPCC. And you are?"

"Ambrose Davids," I replied. CPPCC? Sounded like a remnant of the old Soviet Union. Father would have been looking for conspiracy theories right about now. He'd always had an active imagination.

"Well, Mister Davids," Amari said as she reached into her laptop bag and pulled something out of a side pocket. "I sense you are not quite as sceptical as the rest, so I will give you this." She placed a silver whistle in my hand. "Blow it when you have something we might find interesting."

I stared at the whistle. She had to be kidding me. I suddenly wondered if there was a hidden camera somewhere and my sister would soon show all her friends on YouTube how her brother had fallen for some obscure practical joke.

I looked back at the woman. She raised an

eyebrow at me again. I mumbled my thanks and shoved the whistle deep into my pocket, wondering how much I'd be able to flog it for. Without another word, I turned around and left too. This really had been a waste of time.

❧ ◆ ❧

With twenty quid in my pocket, there would be no eating steak tonight, I thought gloomily as I made my way home on foot. I stopped at a hole-in-the-wall fish and chips shop in Mayfair and ate the greasy fare while walking. I could probably have afforded to take the Tube, but I didn't want to waste the money. No idea when I would get more. Besides, I enjoyed walking, especially now that the rain had cleared up and the wind had died down. Also, I had to admit that these trainers were exceptionally comfortable. At least that was twenty quid well spent.

The light was fading by the time I entered Hyde Park. There were shorter routes home, but I always walked through the park when I had the chance. Something about the trees and the smell of wet grass. It cleared my head.

It was becoming all too apparent that this job interviewing business was not going well. I'm not even sure why they had called me in this morning. They had hardly asked me any questions. Only the one, really - how? How had I made such a crucial mistake? I had shrugged and given them a non-committal answer. The truth would have been too embarrassing, especially in that sterile white boardroom in front of a panel of black-suited and stern-faced brokers.

The sound of a large splash drew me out of my reverie and I stopped short, surprised. I had crossed over into Kensington Gardens and was walking along the path parallel to that part of the Serpentine known as the Long Water. Bushes obscured my view of the lake and I held my breath as I strained to hear what was going on.

Another splash. It sounded too big to be a water bird, and it was too cold and dark for some nutcase in a swimsuit to be out. Gripped by curiosity, I scaled the low fence and pushed past the greenery. My eyes were drawn immediately to a pale figure in the water.

A young woman was floating on her back in the middle of the lake. Her face was pallid under the light of the full moon and her long white dress billowed around her motionless body.

"Help!" I shouted, looking around to see if there was anyone about. Not a soul in sight.

I hesitated at the water's edge. It had never occurred to me that knowing how to swim might one day be a necessary skill. The girl floated, pale and unreachable, like some morbid Lady of the Lake, and me, Arthur, building up the courage to jump in and rescue her.

"Did you off her, then?" a voice behind me said and I nearly jumped out of my skin.

I spun around. It was a teenager, his hoodie pulled low over his eyes so I couldn't make out his entire face, hands thrust deep into his pockets. Probably came here to smoke a joint where no one would see him.

"No, I did not off her," I replied irritably.

"Better call the cops then." He shrugged and turned around, heading towards the path again.

"Hey, wait," I called. "Can you swim?"

"That water looks freezing." He disappeared behind the bushes without a backward glance.

"Unbelievable," I muttered, shaking my head in the direction in which he had left. Then, remembering the need for urgency, I pulled my mobile from my jacket pocket. I dialled Emergency Services and explained the situation. When I ended the call, I turned towards the lake again.

The girl was gone.

❧◆❧

Three hours later, someone handed me a mug of strong coffee while I sat under a blanket and watched the search-and-rescue team fine-comb the lake. They had found no trace of the girl so far, not even a body.

"Mister Davids? May I have a word?"

A woman wearing dark-rimmed hipster glasses stood before me. Her brown hair was swept back into a ponytail and she wore a thick black coat against the evening's cold.

"Detective Inspector Miller, Metropolitan Police," she introduced herself, flashing her badge at me. "Did you say you saw the body of a girl floating in the lake?"

"Yes. I mean no, she wasn't dead." I wrapped my hands around the empty mug, trying unsuccessfully to warm them with the residual heat. I stifled a yawn and wondered when they would let me go home. "I heard splashing before I saw her, so she must have been alive."

"Splashing of a body being dumped into the lake?"

"No." I hesitated. "It sounded... playful."

"Playful."

I nodded, feeling uncharacteristic heat rise to my cheeks. She was looking at me as if she could read all my past offences in my eyes. I resolved yet again to return that dust-covered library book at the back of my closet as soon as possible.

"Did you hear anything else? Any voices? Did the girl cry out for help?"

I shook my head. "No, it was deathly quiet, apart from the splashing. When I saw her, she didn't move, just, sort of, floated. And then she was gone."

Detective Miller's eyes bored into me. "Mister Davids, the police are very busy. We really can't afford to waste time on pranks or hallucinations."

"What?" I spluttered, standing up and dropping the blanket to the floor. "I'm not making this up! There really was a girl in the lake. If I could swim, I would have tried to pull her out myself. Look," I said, dragging a hand through my hair. "There was another kid who saw her. Teenager. Dark hoodie, baggy pants. Ask him, he'll confirm my story."

The detective levelled a stern gaze at me before her face softened. "Alright, Mister Davids. I believe you. I think you should go home now. You look exhausted. We'll contact you if we find anything."

I was exhausted. I nodded gratefully and handed Detective Miller the empty coffee mug. She took it wordlessly, her lips drawn into a thin line and a small frown wrinkling her brow, but I was too tired to pay much attention.

It was after midnight when I pushed the door of my flat closed behind me. I didn't bother to undress before falling onto my bed. I was asleep within seconds.

❧ ◆ ❧

I woke up groggy the next morning with a vein in my temple throbbing like it was a drummer at a Christmas parade. I squinted at the light streaming in through the window where I'd forgotten to close the curtain last night. With a gargantuan effort, I rolled over and peered at my bedside clock. It was past eleven already.

Shit. I'd missed my interview.

I'd really been having the rottenest luck lately.

A flashing light from my mobile lying on the nightstand drew my attention. Two missed calls. I dialled into my voicemail and winced as the nasally voice of Mister Curry, my landlord, blared over the speakerphone.

"Davids! You're a week late on your rent. If I don't get the money by the end of today, I'll have the locks changed, you hear me?"

I deleted the message.

The next call was from Cassie. My sister's perky voice was almost drowned out by background noise. She must have been in a club when she'd called.

"Hey Am, just wanted to know if you're dead or something. Haven't heard from you in a while. Just because that cow left you, doesn't mean your family aren't still here for you. Anyway, call me when you get this message, alright? Love you!"

I groaned as I put the phone down. I wished Cassie hadn't reminded me of 'that cow'. I looked at the picture of Rachel still standing on my bedside table. Then I turned it over, opened the drawer and pushed it in next to the engagement ring I had never had the chance to give her. I slammed the drawer shut, pulled the covers back over me again, rolled over, and went back to sleep.

≈◆≋

It was much later that day when I finally emerged from my apartment. I hadn't bothered to shave or shower and still wore my rumpled suit jacket and white trainers.

I needed to pick up my interview shoes. Although, to be honest, I probably needed a new plan now. No one in the finance industry was going to hire me again; not here in London, and probably nowhere else in the country, either. Still, I wanted my shoes back. They were the last remnants of my old life.

The sky was a pale, empty, grey. The surrounding buildings were grey too, everything from the Houses of Parliament to the high-end stores I was walking towards. It seemed as if the only bit of colour left in the world was the rainbow hanging over the shoe shop.

The bell jingled as I closed the door behind me.

The red-haired man looked up and smiled in recognition.

"Ah, Ambrose Davids. How are the trainers treating you?" he asked in his strong Irish lilt.

"Fine, fine," I said, distracted. I noticed he was wearing a red waistcoat with a four-leaved clover pinned to it. A picture from my youth flashed before my eyes and I inhaled sharply. I'm embarrassed to admit it took me this long to realise it, and even then a few moments passed before I let myself believe it.

I reached into my jacket pocket and pulled out the whistle I had all but forgotten about.

The man's eyes widened in alarm.

"Now hold on, Ambrose," he said, his arms raised as if I were threatening him with a gun. "Let's not do anything rash here. The Council doesn't know I'm here, and I much prefer it that way."

"You're a..." I hesitated. Saying it out loud would be ridiculous. And yet... "Leprechaun?"

The man sighed, his shoulders slumping as he lowered his arms. "I prefer Tuath, but alright then, if you insist. What gave me away? Was it the pin?" he asked, frowning.

"The rainbow," I replied, dazed by the revelation.

"That darn thing," the redhead said, shaking a fist at the ceiling. "I can't tell you how many times I've tried to hide it, but it just keeps popping back up."

"Look, um... Mister Leprechaun..."

The man winced. "My name's Daniel Brady."

"Alright," I said, nodding my head as if this conversation was completely normal. "Daniel, I'll level with you. I'm not sure who the Council is, but a woman told me that if I blow this whistle and bring her anything mythological, or anyone I guess, they'd pay me, and I really need the money right now."

Daniel's face lit up. "If it's money you need, you can have my pot of gold."

I stared at him dumbly.

"And three wishes," he added. "That's a fair trade for my freedom, don't you think?"

"Uh..." I clearly wasn't handling the situation very well.

"Give me a second, I'll be right back," Daniel said, and turned towards a door at the back. He glanced over his shoulder. "Don't blow that whistle, alright? I'll just be two seconds." Then he disappeared into the back.

I don't know what I expected. Him returning with a cast-iron pot filled with gold pieces? A nervous giggle escaped my lips before I could stop it. It was just so absurd. I definitely didn't expect him to return at all, but he was back within seconds, carrying a cheque book.

"Sorry about this," he said as he scribbled on it. "Haven't quite got the hang of Internet banking yet." He grinned as he handed me the cheque.

My eyes bulged. That was a lot of zeros.

"You're giving me all this just so I won't blow this whistle?"

"And three wishes," he said, nodding. "Redeemable anytime you want them. Just three, mind, none of that wishing-for-more-wishes nonsense."

I clutched the cheque, unable to believe my luck. If this were true, everything was about to change. A ray of hope melted the grey from my thoughts.

But something niggled at the back of my mind.

"Who is this Council?" I asked. "And why are you afraid of them?"

"The Elder Council," Daniel replied, his voice lowered, as if afraid they might hear him if he spoke any louder. "They mean well, I'm sure, but I don't need their help. I can get by on my own. I much prefer freedom over safety. Don't you agree, Ambrose?"

"Sure," I said, entirely unsure and none the wiser.

"Thanks," I said, lifting the cheque up. I turned around to go, startled by the bell as I opened the door again.

"Hey Ambrose," Daniel called. "Don't forget your shoes."

❧ ◆ ☙

The full moon gazed down on me by the time I stumbled out of the pub. After the best meal I'd had in ages, and a few too many beers to wash it down with, I was in the mood for a stroll.

I had never been as nervous as I had been while standing in front of the glass window at the bank, waiting for the cashier to cash my cheque. I was certain something would go wrong. She'd look at it and laugh at me for falling for a scam, or phone security and have me arrested or something. But as I stood there, sweating through my shirt and rumpling my unwashed hair even more, the lady had efficiently and disinterestedly completed all the necessary admin and sent me on my way again.

I couldn't believe my luck had finally changed.

The first thing I did was transfer the rent money, just to get Mister Curry off my back. Then, the financier in me won over and I sensibly paid off all my student debts as well. I felt like Atlas without the world on my shoulders.

I considered buying a sports car next. Instead, I went to the nearest pub to celebrate.

The brisk evening air had sobered me up a bit by the time I reached the lake in Hyde Park on my way home again. I shuddered at the memory of last night, which seemed surreal now. Could I have imagined the young woman in the water? It had probably been an illusion conjured up by my stressed out mind. An overactive imagination did run in the family, after all.

Then I heard splashing again.

I was over the fence before I'd had time to think about it.

The girl I had seen floating in the lake last night was sitting on a rocky outcrop, bare feet tracing circles in the water. Pale blond hair flowed down her back in wet ringlets and a lacy white dress straight out of the Victorian era clung to a figure that had me swallowing nervously. Her skin was almost translucent in the bright light of the full moon. She must have heard me, because she looked up from her reverie and fixed eyes the colour of a morning mist upon me. I felt my heart rate quicken and my knees turn to jelly. She was beautiful. I wanted nothing more in that instant than to walk over, take her in my arms and kiss her until we were both gasping for breath. I took a tentative step towards her.

The girl slipped gracefully into the water.

"Wait!" I said before I could stop myself.

To my surprise, she turned towards me again, her pale hair fanning out behind her in the water.

"Who are you?" I asked, slowly advancing, hoping not to startle her again. She remained in the water, watching me closely, but did not retreat. "I mean you no harm," I said as I reached the edge of the lake. I bent down and sat on my haunches, all fear of the water forgotten as I stared into those entrancing eyes.

The girl remained silent, but she stood up in the waist deep water, rivulets running down her wet dress. She smiled enticingly and beckoned me closer with one finger as she slowly walked backwards, deeper into the lake.

I needed no further urging. I was in the water before I knew it. Somewhere in the back of my mind, I vaguely realised that it was getting deeper and deeper - it was up to my chest now - but I hardly noticed. I cared even less. I could almost touch her.

She reached her hands out to me, longingly, and

I stretched towards her. Our fingertips caressed.

And then the girl grabbed my wrist and pulled me under the water.

I gulped water as my head went under the surface. The shock forced my eyes open and I watched, horrified, as the moonlight retreated and we plunged deeper and deeper into the lake.

I struggled, tasting bile, and flailed wildly, but her grip was like iron. I could not escape.

And then my hand was free and I was floating, floating. I looked around. The girl was gone and I was hovering in darkness. Far away, a dim light beckoned. I kicked feebly, half-heartedly.

I was drowning.

Find the full novel here:

BOOKS2READ.COM/MYTHHUNTER

www.ingramcontent.com/pod-product-compliance
Lightning Source LLC
Chambersburg PA
CBHW052007220626
47052CB00004B/1129